Gwyneth Rees is half Welsh and half English and grew up in Scotland. She went to Glasgow University and qualified as a doctor in 1990. She is a child and adolescent psychiatrist but has now stopped practising so that she can write full-time. She is the author of the bestselling Fairies series (*Fairy Dust*, *Fairy Treasure*, *Fairy Dreams*, *Fairy Gold* and *Fairy Rescue*), *Cosmo and the Magic Sneeze* and *Cosmo and the Great Witch Escape*, and *Mermaid Magic*, as well as several books for older readers. She lives in London with her two cats.

Visit www.gwynethrees.com

Amanda Li is a writer and editor who has worked in children's publishing for many years. She lives in London with her family.

Gwyneth Rees

Cosmo's

Book of

Spooky

Fun

Compiled by Amanda Li

Illustrated by Sam Hearn

MACMILLAN CHILDREN'S BOOKS

First published 2007 by Macmillan Children's Books
a division of Macmillan Publishers Limited
20 New Wharf Road, London N1 9RR
Basingstoke and Oxford
www.panmacmillan.com

Associated companies throughout the world

ISBN: 978-0-330-45123-9

1 3 5 7 9 8 6 4 2

A CIP catalogue record for this book is available from
the British Library.

Typeset by Nigel Hazle
Printed and bound in Great Britain by Mackays of Chatham plc, Kent

Contents

Cast of Characters

Sybil   Scarlett   India

Mia   Cosmo   Mephisto

Cleo Cattrap

Euphemia

Selina Slaughter

Albert-of-the-Street

Goody Two-Shoes

Felina

2

From Gwyneth Rees

Cosmo the kitten would love this book – if only he could read Human. As you're bound to know if you've read my stories about him, Cosmo is very good at solving puzzles and he especially likes mysteries that involve witches. In *Cosmo and the Magic Sneeze* he has to find out which spell Sybil the bad witch is making so that he can stop her from using it. And in *Cosmo and the Great Witch Escape* he has to solve the mystery of who is stealing the special magical toenails from newborn witch-babies.

Cosmo has lots of friends who help him, and you'll find them all in this book. For instance, there's his best friend, Mia, who lives next door (and who might become his girlfriend when they get a bit older!), and her mother, Felina, who is a very clever professor cat. He also has a two-legged friend, Scarlett the witch-girl, who is eager to stop Sybil too. And as well as his friends there are his parents – Mephisto and India – who (like all good parents) are very proud of him and think he is the most perfect kitten in the whole world.

I sometimes get asked if any of the characters

3

in my Cosmo stories are based on real cats! Well, some of them are!

When I was a child growing up in Scotland, I had a Siamese cat called Tani, so in *Cosmo and the Magic Sneeze* I put in a Siamese witch-cat called Tani, who rescues Cosmo's friend Mia from the jaws of a nasty dog. (I used to dress up the real Tani in dolls' clothes and wheel her about in my dolls' pram, but I don't think the Tani in my book would be up for that!)

In *Cosmo and the Great Witch Escape* Tani appears again, only this time she has two Siamese kittens called Hagnus and Matty. If I tell you that the two cats I have now are called Magnus and Hattie, then I think you can guess who those kittens are based on!

There's another cat I 'borrowed' from real life because I think she has such a fantastic name. She's a very ditzy tabby cat called Tigger-Louise, who used to live in the next street to me in London, but who now lives in the countryside (where I hear she has shortened her name to Tigs).

A very important cat character in *Cosmo and the Great Witch Escape* is called Cleo Cattrap. Cleo

4

is based on a real cat called Oscar, who I met when I visited a little girl I know called Megan. Oscar – a long-haired, very fluffy, silver-tabby, *almost* Persian cat – used to love having his fur dried under the hairdryer when he first went to live with Megan and her mum. Since most cats *hate* hairdryers (my two certainly do!) I thought that made him a very special cat and I decided to give him a starring role in my second Cosmo book!

And last but not least, you might want to know who Cosmo himself is based on. Well, the truth is, I didn't really base him on any cat in particular, but, believe it or not, Cosmo is a bit like me. You see, we both love puzzles!

This is Cosmo's very own activity book and it's packed full of puzzles and other fun things to do. So climb aboard now, hold on to your (witch's) hat and take a whizzy broomstick ride with Cosmo through this cauldron full of spooky fun!

Witches - Good or Bad?

Can you tell the good witches (Scarlett) from the bad witches (Euphemia)? Count each type of witch and write the numbers of goodies and baddies in the clouds below.

There are
___
goodies

There are
___
baddies

7

Scarlett's Sound Spell

Scarlett has mixed up all these animal
sounds with her magic spell. Can you match
them back to the right animals by drawing
lines?

Croak!

Hisssssss!

Miaow!

Woof! Woof!

Squeak!

Too-whit
too-whoo!

Cosmo's Crossword

Think you know all about cats? Try this crossword and find out!

Across

2. One of a cat's favourite foods. Can be a bit smelly!
4. A witch sometimes needs her witch-cat to do this. It helps her make her magic spell.
5. The name for a baby cat.

Down

1. Cats usually like to chase these little animals.
3. The noise a cat makes.
4. Cats have sharp claws and they usually enjoy a good _ _ _ _ _ _ _ .
   Especially when they've got fleas!

Dot-to-dot

Join the dots to find everyone's favourite witch-cat.

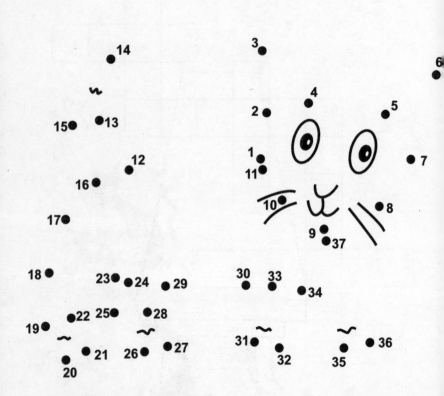

Catwalk Creation

Cleo Cattrap's in town and he's looking for the cutest cats and kittens around! Can you draw a gorgeous cat on the catwalk below?

13

Spot the Difference

Can you spot the seven differences between these pictures of Cosmo and Sybil?

B

What's on Witch TV?

There's nothing witches like more than a relaxing TV programme. Can you match the title of the TV show to the correct screen?

D Time for
Witch
NEWS

C *Sporty Witches*

E It's Witch Cookery!

Write your answers here:

1 ⬡ 2 ⬡ 3 ⬡ 4 ⬡ 5 ⬡

17

Frog Fun

Read what each frog is saying and draw the correct number of spots on its back.

19

Match the Hats

Can you join up the matching pairs of witches' hats?

Witch-cat Jokes

Why does a witch need a cat to help her?
She wants to find the purr-fect spell.

What happened when Sybil tried
to change a cat into a sea-monster?
She got an octo-puss.

What happened when she tried to
change a cat into a garden tool?
She got a lawn miaower.

What do you call a witch's
cat wearing wellies?
Puss in Boots.

Cat Scramble

All the mixed-up words are parts of Cosmo's body. Can you unscramble them and write the words on the spaces below? Then draw a line to the right part of the body.

e r a

_ _ _

s e o n

_ _ _ _

a l t i

_ _ _ _

y e e

_ _ _

w a p

_ _ _

s h i w e r k

<u>w</u> <u>h</u> _ _ _ _ _

23

Cauldron Creature Wordsearch

Which creatures can you find in this witch's cauldron?

L	I	T	M	E	S	M	E
I	C	P	O	R	T	S	R
Z	R	O	U	A	L	B	E
A	U	H	S	P	D	L	D
R	L	N	E	W	T	G	I
D	F	A	K	E	J	M	P
R	O	U	E	C	O	Z	S
E	G	B	D	N	R	A	T

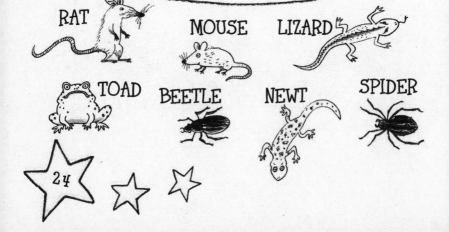

RAT   MOUSE   LIZARD

TOAD   BEETLE   NEWT   SPIDER

Colour by Numbers

Use the colour key to colour in this picture.

✏ 1 Black ✏ 2 White ✏ 3 Green ✏ 4 Brown ✏ 5 Dark Blue

25

Sybil's Spell

Sybil the Witch has made a list of ingredients for her new spell. Read the list, then write the number of creatures she will need in the boxes opposite.

Sybil's Spell Ingredients

Four fat frogs

Six slithering snakes

One rancid rat

Seven scuttling spiders

Two terrifying toads

Eight eerie earwigs

Witchy Wordsnake

Can you find the witchy words listed below in the grid opposite? Use a pencil to trace them. The words form one continuous line, snaking up and down, backwards and forwards, but never diagonally.

WAND
CAULDRON
HAT
CLOAK
SPELL
MAGIC
BROOMSTICK
CAT
WIZARD
POTION
ENCHANT
TOAD
MICE

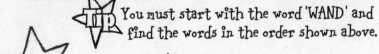

TIP You must start with the word 'WAND' and find the words in the order shown above.

28

Start

W	A	C	E	A	O	T
D	N	I	M	D	N	T
C	A	U	L	D	A	H
O	L	C	T	R	N	C
A	K	S	A	O	E	N
L	E	P	H	N	I	O
L	A	T	Z	A	T	O
M	C	W	I	R	D	P
A	K	C	I	T	S	M
G	I	C	B	R	O	O

29

Shadow Match

Can you match each cat and its shadow?

Nifty Names

Cosmo is a great name for a cat, and just like the word 'cat' it begins with a 'c'. Can you think of good names for each of these animals? Each name must begin with the same letter as the animal.

Ollie

owl

_____

mouse

_____ bat

spider _____

_____ frog

Dotty Drawing

Colour in the dotted shapes to find a spooky creature of the night.

Dot-to-dot

Join the dots to find the spider's home.

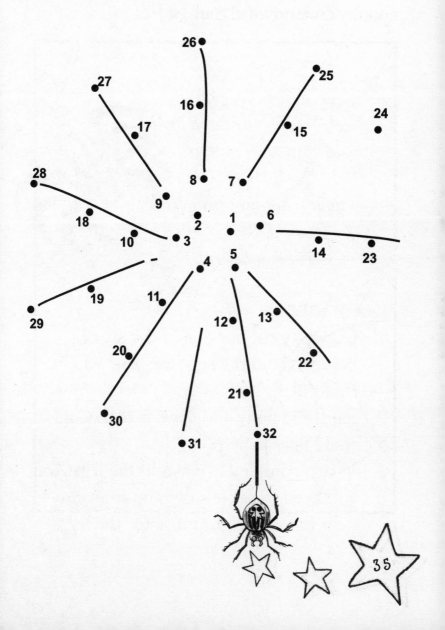

Make a Bouncing Spider

This spider will scare off any witch who dares to come near your bedroom!

You will need:
A cardboard egg box
Black/brown paint and brush
A thin piece of elastic
Scissors
Four black pipe cleaners
Glue
Paper and pens

How to make:

1. Carefully cut out one of the six egg holders from the egg box. This will be the spider's body.
2. Paint the body and leave it to dry on some newspaper.
3. When completely dry, add the legs. You will need to ask a grown up for some help to make eight holes for the legs

with a pen. Cut lengths of pipe cleaner about 5 cm long and poke them through the sides of the body. Bend the ends of the pipe cleaner inside the body to hold them securely.

Bend pipe cleaners inside the body

4. Now add some eyes. Draw some scary eyes on a piece of paper and colour them in. Cut them out and stick them on the front of the spider. Why not add fangs for that extra fear factor?

5. Finally, make a small hole in the top of the spider. Thread your piece of elastic through the hole and tie a knot inside the egg holder. If you don't have any elastic, use wool, string or thread instead.
6. Now you have a super-scary spider that just loves to bounce!

Scuttling Spiders

Look very carefully at these scary spiders. One of them is not a real spider. Can you work out which one it is?

remember — all spiders have eight legs.

More Witch-cat Jokes

What do you call a witch-cat who is better at making spells than her witch?
An ex-purr-t.

 What do witch-cats watch on TV?
The daily mews.

How do you start a race of itchy witch-cats?
One, two, flea!

What goes 'now you see it, now you don't, now you see it, now you don't'?
A black cat on a zebra crossing.

Complete Cosmo

Here comes Cosmo! Can you draw the missing lines to complete the picture?

Odd One Out 1

Look carefully at the pictures below. Can you circle the picture in each set of three that is different from the others?

1a

1b

1c

2a

2b

2c

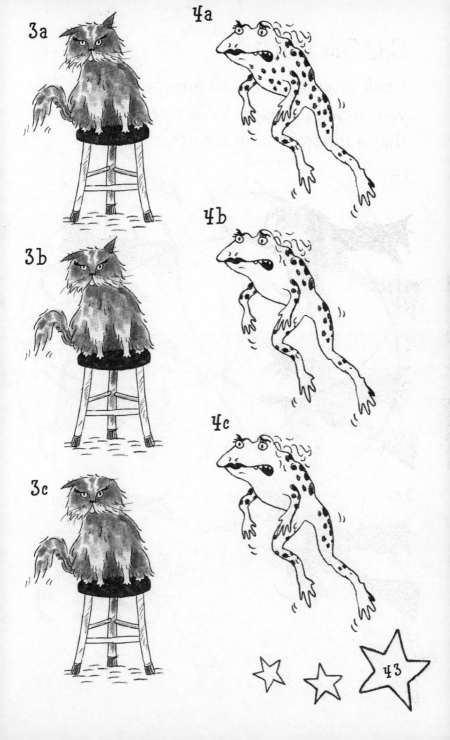

3a

3b

3c

4a

4b

4c

43

Which Witch?

Which of these witches has made the spooky spell?

A

B

C

44

Cage Maze

Evil witch Sybil has locked Scarlett, Mia and Albert-of-the-street into a cage. Can you help them find the way out?

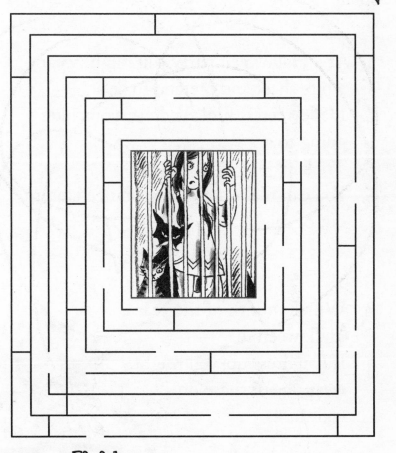

Finish

45

Halloween Crossword

Halloween is the witches' favourite night of the year. How much do you know about it?

Across

1. At a Halloween party you might wear a white sheet and pretend to be a _ _ _ _ _ .
3. Halloween is fun! And everyone likes going to a _ _ _ _ _ .
5. Trick or _ _ _ _ _ ?
6. You can make a glowing orange lantern out of this.

Down

2. Which month of the year is Halloween in?
4. If you dress up, you might wear one of these on your face.

Yeuch!

Selina Slaughter has created a really revolting spell – just look at some of the ingredients she's using! Can you create a spell that's just as revolting as Selina's?

Donkey Dribble

Write the names of your ingredients on these jars and bottles.

49

Witch Jokes

What has six legs and flies?
A witch giving her cat a lift.

What do witches do at school?
Spell-ing tests.

What do witches wear in the summertime?
Open-toad sandals.

Why do witches fly on broomsticks?
Because vacuum cleaners are much too heavy.

Colour Euphemia

Use lots of witchy colours to colour in this picture of the evil Euphemia.

Euphemia's hair is green.

Dot-to-dot

Join the dots to find a creature that witch-cats like to chase.

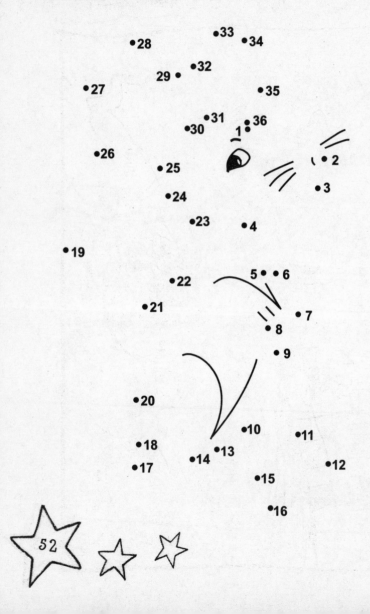

Colour by Numbers

Use the colour key here to colour the picture in.

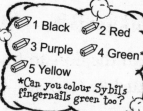

1 Black 2 Red
3 Purple 4 Green*
5 Yellow
*Can you colour Sybil's fingernails green too?

53

Spooky Secret Code

Cosmo's left you a secret message. Can you work it out by using the spooky picture code below? Write each letter in the space as you find it.

A · J · S
B · K · T
C · L · U
D · M · V
E · N · W
F · O · X
G · P · Y
H · Q · Z
I · R

54

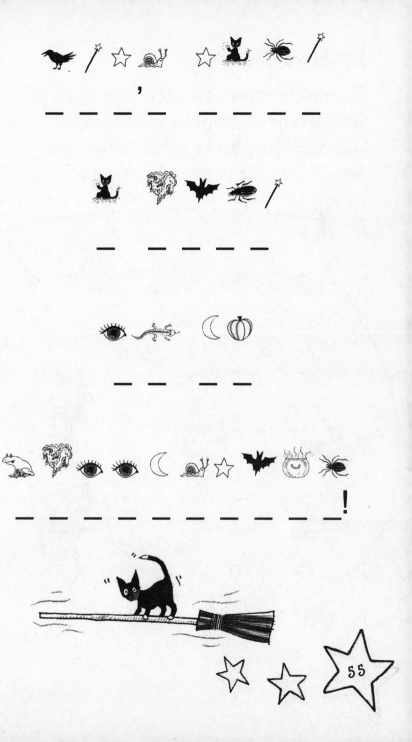

55

Cauldron Rhyme

Euphemia's been making a rhyming spell with lots of different ingredients. Can you draw lines between the things that rhyme with each other, e.g. slug and bug.

Design a Witch's Outfit

Scarlett is off to a witches' party. Can you create an outfit for her? Try some interesting witchy patterns. Don't forget her shoes!

Kitty Know-how

How much do you know about cat behaviour? Below are six important things to know about cats. Can you fill in the missing letters to complete the words?

Things cats like:

1. <u>m</u> _ _ <u>k</u>

2. <u>f</u> _ _ <u>s</u> <u>h</u>

Things cats do:

3. <u>s</u> _ <u>r</u> _ _ <u>c</u> <u>h</u>

4. <u>l</u> _ _ <u>c</u> <u>k</u>

Noises cats make:

5. _ i _ o w

6. p _ r _

There is one very important thing that witch-cats do to help witches make their spells. Do you know what it is?

7. _ _ e e z e

59

Memory Test

Cosmo and his cat friends are trying to make hairballs for a magic spell. Look carefully at the picture, then cover it up with a piece of paper. Can you remember enough to answer the true/false questions below?

True or false? Tick the box

1. There are seven cats in the picture.
   True ☐   False ☐
2. Cosmo is looking into a bucket.
   True ☐   False ☐
3. One cat is sitting on the hand dryer.
   True ☐   False ☐
4. The cat sitting in the sink looks very happy.
   True ☐   False ☐
5. Two cats are coming in through the window.
   True ☐   False ☐

Pawprint Puzzle

Professor Felina has lost her cat encyclopedia. Can you help her find it? Trace the pawprints with your finger to find the right trail.

Dotty Drawing

Colour in the dotted shapes to find a creature that could be lurking in a witch's cauldron.

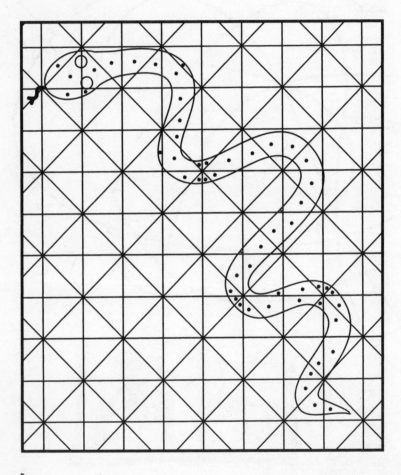

Sybil's Shopping List

Witch Sybil's shopping list has got wet in the rain and some of the letters have been washed away. Can you complete the words so she can finish her shopping?

Shopping list

1. S _ _ _ ders' webs
2. R _ t's droppings
3. Fr _ _ s' l _ gs
4. D _ _ key dribble
5. Polar bear b _ rps
6. B _ _ ds' feathers

Cauldron Counting 1

Which group of frogs belongs in which cauldron? Count the frogs and draw a line to the correctly numbered cauldron.

1

2

3

4

5

3

7

5

8

4

A

B

C

D

E

67

Draw the Missing Half

Can you complete this picture of Scarlett?
Then colour the picture in.

More Witch Jokes

What goes 'cackle, cackle, bonk'?
A witch laughing her head off.

What noise do witches make as
they fly past?
Brroom, brroom!

What would you do if a witch in a
pointy hat sat in front of you in the
cinema?
Miss the film.

What do witches wrap their
presents with?
Spellotape.

Witch's Wardrobe

Everything in Selina Slaughter's wardrobe has got an exact double. Can you match them up by drawing a line between the two things? There will be one thing left over. What is it?

Magical Rhymes

Can you find the right word to complete these rhymes?

1. Can you see Cosmo, he's gone out at
      night,
      His body is black but his paws
      are _ _ _ _ _ .

2. A witch is a person who owns a witch-
      cat,
      She makes magic spells and she wears a
      big _ _ _ .

3. Abracadabra! Let's make a spell,
      Whoops, it's gone wrong,
        there's a terrible _ _ _ _ _ .

4. Into the cauldron goes a newt's tail,
      Now throw in a spider, a slug and
      a _ _ _ _ _ .

5. There on her broomstick, see the witch fly,
   High in the clouds, up, up in the _ _ _ .

6. Could that be a witch? You may not have seen,
   That under her cloak, her toenails are _ _ _ _ _ .

green

white

snail

sky

smell

hat

Make a Ghostly Drinking Straw

Make your drink into a spine-tingling treat by using this spook-tacular straw. Great for spooky sleepovers!

You will need:
A drinking straw
A piece of paper
Scissors
Pens for colouring

How to make:

1. Trace the spooky ghost opposite on to your piece of paper. Colour it in.

2. Cut the ghost out carefully.

3. Make a cut in the mouth on the dotted line (you may need a grown-up to help with this).

4. Slide the ghost on to your straw. There you have it – a drink just right for a witch!

Colour Scarlett and Cosmo

 Scarlett has dark hair. Cosmo is black with white paws and a white tip on his tail.

Mouse Maze

This mouse is trying to find his way home. Which trail should he follow? If he takes the wrong one he might end up in a bubbling witch's cauldron!

A   B   C

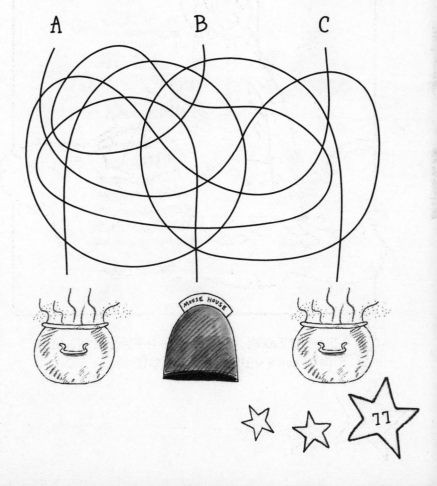

MOUSE HOUSE

77

It's Behind You!

Can you identify Cosmo and some of the people and cats he knows – from behind? Write the letter in the cauldron next to each name.

A

C

B

TIP If you're not sure, look at the pictures on page 1, where you can see them from the front.

D

E

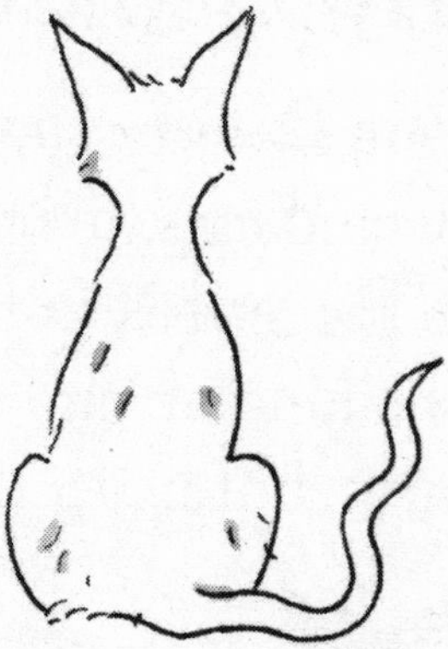

India

Scarlett

Cosmo

Mia

Sybil

Mephisto

F

Spooky Wordsnake

Can you find the spooky things listed below in the grid opposite? Use a pencil to trace them. The words form one continuous line, snaking up and down, backwards and forwards, but never diagonally.

WIZARD

WITCH

GHOST

MONSTER

VAMPIRE

GOBLIN

TROLL

ZOMBIE

BAT

 You must start with the word 'WIZARD' and find the words in the order shown above.

Start

W	I	T	C	H
I	W	T	S	G
Z	D	M	O	H
A	R	O	A	T
T	S	N	B	E
E	R	V	A	I
B	O	G	M	B
L	I	E	P	M
T	N	R	I	O
R	O	L	L	Z

81

Spiders' Web Game

Join all the spiders up in the correct order, from 1–20, by drawing a line between each one.

Start

82

Draw a Witch

Why not make up your very own witch?
Scary or sweet, it's up to you! If you're
stuck for ideas, the pictures below might
help.

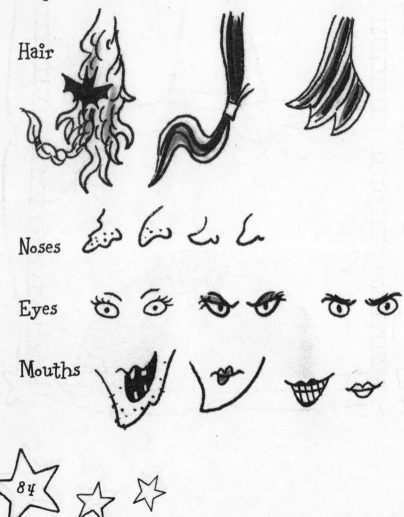

Hair

Noses

Eyes

Mouths

85

Witch Words

Unscramble the letters in the witches' hats to find five things that are very important to witches. Write the words below the hats.

1. t a c

_ _ _ _

2. w d a n

_ _ _ _ _

3. s l e l p

_ _ _ _ _ _

4. a g i m c

_ _ _ _ _

5. m o o s t r b i k c

_ _ _ _ _ _ _ _ _

Dot-to-dot

Join the dots to find a spooky person.

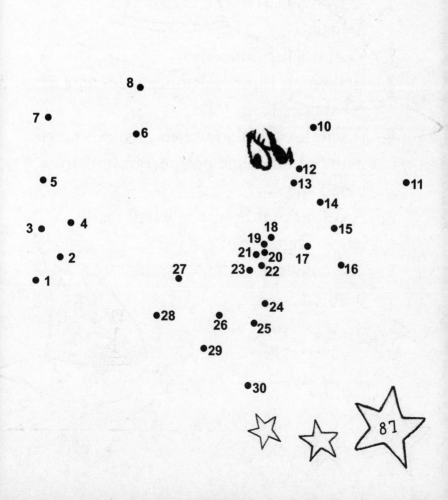

Cosmo's Colour Wordsearch

Read the clues below to find six colours in the grid opposite. The colours are written across, down, backwards, forwards and diagonally. Why not use your favourite colour to shade in each word as you find it?

1. The colour of a witch's hair and toenails. _ _ _ _ _ _
2. Cosmo's fur is mostly _ _ _ _ _ .
3. Evil witch Euphemia once made lots of cat statues from solid _ _ _ _ .
4. A witch-cat's blood turns green if mixed with Sybil's magic potion, but human blood stays _ _ _ .
5. A colour that Sybil the witch really hates – but lots of girls love. _ _ _ _
6. The colour of India, Cosmo's mother. _ _ _ _ _ _

G	A	G	R	E	E	N	B	E
A	B	O	I	N	K	N	I	P
C	E	L	D	O	U	F	G	I
D	L	D	C	N	K	U	E	M
K	A	P	M	C	F	D	T	O
M	I	Q	A	S	E	A	I	R
L	R	L	T	D	I	M	H	N
E	B	N	S	H	E	Q	W	J
O	V	G	B	K	R	P	U	

89

Cauldron Counting 2

Here are four witches' cauldrons. Count the creatures in each one and write the number in the box beside it. Which one has got the most creatures in it?

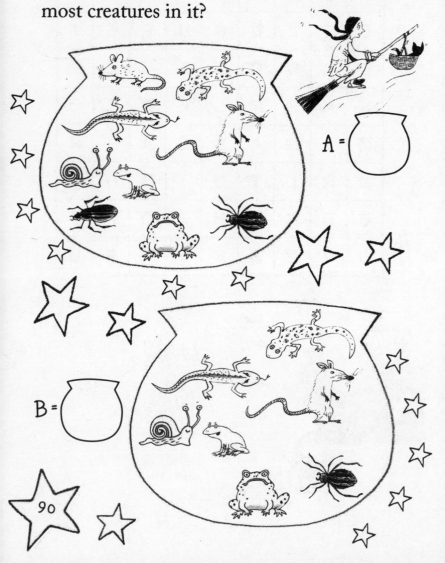

A =

B =

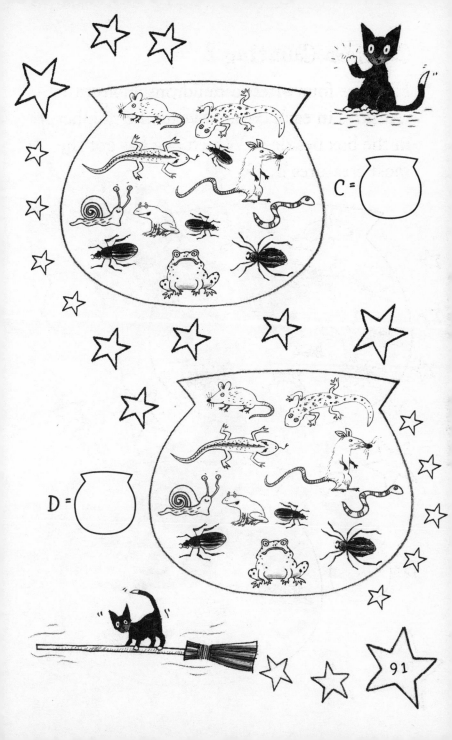

C =

D =

Spot the Difference

Can you spot seven differences between these pictures of Selina Slaughter?

Spooky Picture Crossword

Can you complete this spooky crossword by looking at the pictures and writing the names in the spaces?

Across

2

3

4

5

Down

1

2

6

94

Create an Ancient Spell

Make this authentic-looking witch's spell and fool your friends!

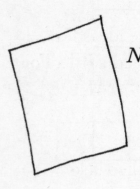

You will need:
A sheet of paper
Newspaper or protective cloth
A used tea bag
A saucer or cup of water
Black/brown felt-tip pen
Lots of ideas!

How to make:

1. First, crumple the sheet of paper into a ball, then flatten it. Gently tear the edges of the paper to give it a really ancient look.

2. Lay the paper on to a sheet of newspaper or cloth, then dip the tea bag into the

96

water and wipe it all over the surface of the paper to give it a brown, parchmenty look.

3. While the paper is drying, work out some ideas for your spell. First you'll need a title. For example: A SPELL TO MAKE YOU INVISIBLE, or HOW TO TURN A FROG INTO A PRINCE. Then think of a list of ingredients, the yuckier the better! Write some simple instructions – perhaps you'll need to say some magic words while mixing the ingredients? Write your ideas down.

4. Finally, in your best handwriting, carefully copy out your magic spell on to the parchment. Use a brown or black pen.

5. Abracadabra! A real witch's spell to amaze your friends.

Barny Broomsticks

Watch out! Cosmo's riding his broomstick and he's out of control. Which of these crazy broomstick trails belongs to him?

Colour by Numbers

Can you colour this picture of Goody Two-Shoes, Scarlett and baby Spike, using the guide below?

🖍1 Red 🖍2 Blue 🖍3 Brown 🖍4 Black 🖍5 Yellow

🖍6 Green 🖍7 Pink

Find the Witch's Shadow

A spell has gone wrong and all these witches have lost their shadows. Can you match them up again?

1

2

3

4

5

100

A

B

C

D

E

Odd One Out 2

Look carefully at the pictures below. Can you circle the picture on each set of three that is different from the others?

1a   1b   1c

2a   2b   2c

3a

3b

3c

4a

4b

4c

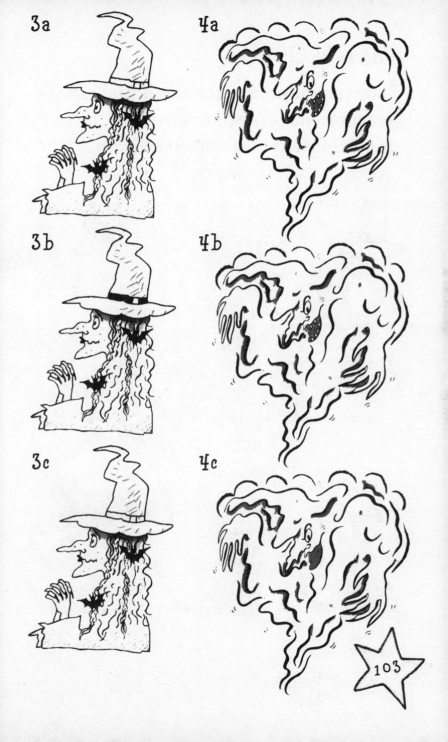

103

Cosmo Wordsnake

Use a pencil to trace the words below in the grid opposite. The words form one continuous line, snaking up and down, backwards and forwards, but never diagonally.

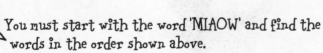

MIAOW

FLEA

HAIRBALL

KITTEN

BROOMSTICK

WITCH

CLAWS

FUR

TAIL

SNEEZE

PAWS

 Tip You must start with the word 'MIAOW' and find the words in the order shown above.

Start

M	S	W	A	P
I	A	O	Z	E
L	F	W	E	E
E	A	L	S	N
A	H	I	A	T
I	R	F	U	R
A	B	S	W	A
L	L	K	C	L
N	E	I	H	C
B	T	T	I	T
R	M	S	W	K
O	O	T	I	C

105

Dot-to-dot

Join the dots to find a member of Cosmo's family.

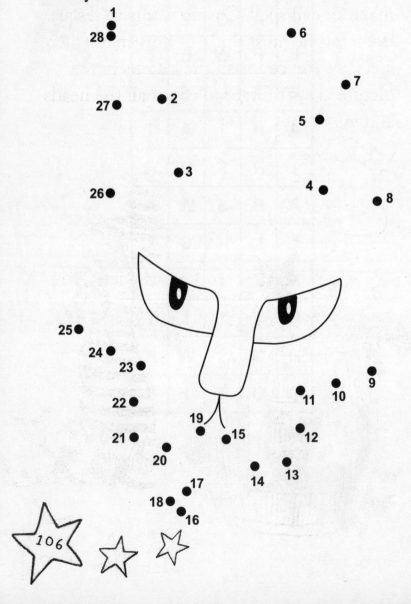

106

Counting Kittens

Sybil the witch has lured all these kittens into a barrel because she needs them to make an evil spell. Cosmo wants to rescue them but he must find out how many there are. Can you count all the kittens in the picture? Don't forget to count all the heads and tails.

There are _____ kittens to rescue

Free fish for all kittens!

Where Are the Witches?

It's Halloween and the night sky is full of witches flying around. How many witches have brought their cats with them? Count and write the numbers in the boxes.

There are
___
with cats

There are
___
without cats

109

Cosmo Jokes

What do you call it when Cosmo
falls off his broomstick?
A cat-astrophe.

What's Cosmo's favourite bedtime
story?
He likes a furry tale.

What does Cosmo like for
breakfast?
Mice Krispies.

What's Cosmo and Mia's favourite
game?
Mew-sical chairs.

110

Sybil's Spell

Cosmo and Mephisto have been helping
Sybil to make one of her magic spells.
What has she created this time? Use your
imagination to draw the thing she has
made, then colour it in.

Make a Cosmo Cat Mask

Pretend to be everyone's favourite witch cat with this purr-fect mask.

You will need:

A piece of thin card (a cereal box is ideal)
A piece of paper
Scissors
A drinking straw
Colouring pens or paints
Sticky tape/glue
4–6 short pieces of wool or 3 pipe cleaners
Glitter (optional)

How to make:

1. Trace the cat template opposite on to a piece of paper and cut it out. Place the shape on to the card and draw around it. Now cut out your mask.

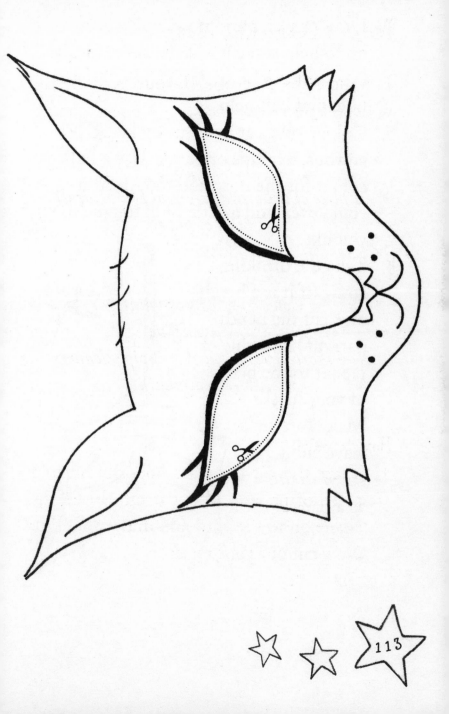

2. Draw the eyes and nose. Ask a grown-up to help you cut out the holes for the eyes as it can be tricky. Making a small hole first will help.

3. Colour your cat mask using black crayons, felt-tips or paints. Use a light colour for the nose and mouth. You could even add a little pink tongue if you like.

4. Take the drinking straw (if it is a bendy one, cut the bendy part off) and glue or tape it to the back of your mask. Make sure to leave enough straw to use as a handle.

5. Finally, glue Cosmo's whiskers to the front of the mask. Use two or three strands of wool on each cheek. (If using pipe cleaners, cut them in half and use tape to stick them behind the mask). If you have some glitter or sequins, dab a little glue above Cosmo's eyes and add some sparkle.

6. Now you have it – a great mask to 'amews' all your friends!

Design a Magic Carpet

Scarlett and Cosmo are flying through the sky on a magic-carpet adventure. Can you create a pattern on the carpet that would suit a witch? Think moons, stars, bats or anything else you fancy!

Dotty Drawing

Colour the dotted shapes to find a creature associated with witches.

What Do They Need?

Each of these characters needs something. Look at the three objects next to them and circle the correct one.

A

I need something to read.

B

I need to fly somewhere fast.

118

Odd One Out 3

Look carefully at these four pictures of Mia.
Which one is different from the rest?
Circle the picture when you have found it.

Colouring Fun

Colour in this picture of Scarlett and her mother, Goody Two-Shoes.

Cats, Bats and Rats!

This witch's room is full of pets – and as you can see, she likes cats, bats and rats. Can you count how many there are of each creature and write the number in the correct box?

There are:

 cats

 bats

 rats

Are You Crazy About Cosmo?

Do you love reading stories about Cosmo the cat and his adventures in the world of witches? Then find out how much you know about Cosmo's world in this spellbinding quiz!

1. What is the name of Cosmo's mother?
    ☐ India
    ☐ China
    ☐ Africa

2. What colour are a witch's toenails?
    ☐ Purple
    ☐ Red
    ☐ Green

3. What would happen to a witch if she tried to harm a cat?

☐ She'd turn into a mouse

☐ She'd become invisible

☐ She'd go up in a puff of smoke

4. How many hairballs does Selina Slaughter need to collect for her evil spell?

☐ 10

☐ 50

☐ 100

5. What do witches need cats to do in order to make their magic spells?
   ☐ Sneeze
   ☐ Cough
   ☐ Yawn

6. Cosmo is a black cat – but which part of his body is white?
   ☐ Ears
   ☐ Paws
   ☐ Whiskers

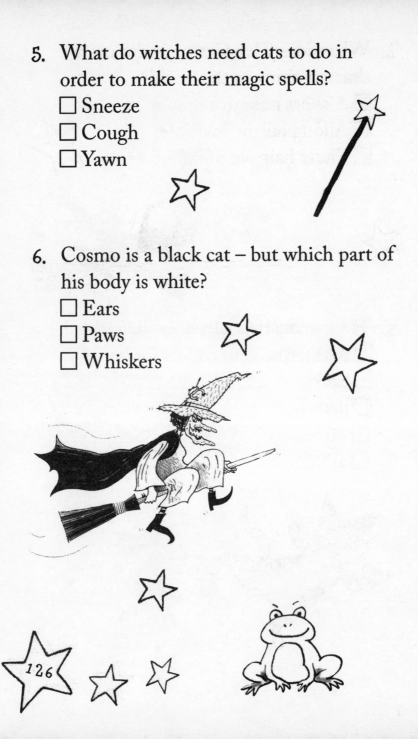

7. What does Cleo Cattrap want more than anything in the world?
   ☐ A short nose
   ☐ A long tail
   ☐ Fluffy hair

8. What is Scarlett's baby brother called?
   ☐ Mike
   ☐ Spike
   ☐ Jake

127

Answers

Page 6 – Witches – Good or Bad?
There are 8 goodies and 7 baddies.

Page 8 – Scarlett's Sound Spell
Croak! – frog, Hissssssss! – snake, Miaow! – cat,
Woof! Woof! – dog, Squeak! – mouse,
Too-whit too-whoo! – owl

**Page 10 – Cosmo's
Crossword**

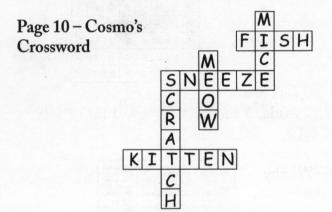

**Page 14 – Spot the
Difference**

Page 16 – What's on Witch TV?
1. D, 2. C, 3. E, 4. A, 5. B

Page 23 – Cat Scramble
era – ear, seon – nose, alti – tail, yee – eye,
wap – paw, shiwerk – whisker

**Page 24 – Cauldron
Creature Wordsearch**

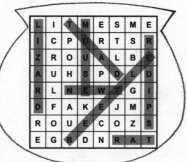

Page 26 – Sybil's Spell
7 spiders, 2 toads, 8 earwigs, 4 frogs, 1 rat,
6 snakes.

**Page 28 – Witchy
Wordsnake**

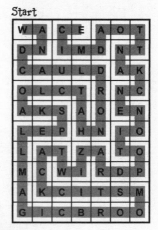

Page 30 – Shadow Match
1. B, 2. F, 3. A, 4. E, 5. D, 6. C

Page 39 – Scuttling Spiders

Page 42 – Odd One Out 1
1a, 2c, 3c, 4a

Page 44 – Which Witch?
Witch A

Page 45 – Cage Maze

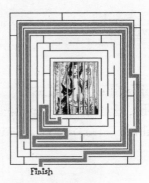

Finish

Page 46 – Halloween Crossword

Page 54 – Spooky Secret Code
LET'S TAKE A RIDE ON MY BROOMSTICK!

Page 56 – Cauldron Rhyme
frog – dog, wizard – lizard, moon – spoon, tree – bee,
bat – cat

Page 58 – Kitty Know-how
1. milk, 2. fish, 3. scratch, 4. lick, 5. miaow, 6. purr,
7. sneeze

Page 60 – Memory Test
1. False, six, 2. True, 3. True, 4. False, 5. False, one

Page 62 – Pawprint Puzzle
Trail C

Page 65 – Sybil's Shopping List
1. Spiders' webs, 2. Rat's droppings, 3. Frogs' legs,
4. Donkey dribble, 5. Polar bear burps, 6. Birds'
feathers

Page 66 – Cauldron Counting 1
1. D, 2. B, 3. A, 4. E, 5. C

Page 70 – Witch's Wardrobe
The wand

Page 72 – Magical Rhymes
1. white, 2. hat, 3. smell, 4. snail, 5. sky, 6. green

Page 77 – Mouse Maze
Trail B

Page 78 – It's Behind You!
A. Cosmo, B. Mia, C. Sybil, D. Scarlett, E. India,
F. Mephisto

**Page 80 – Spooky
Wordsnake**

Page 86 – Witch Words
1. cat, 2. wand, 3. spell, 4. magic, 5. broomstick

**Page 88 – Cosmo's
Colour Wordsearch**

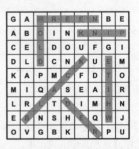

Page 90 – Cauldron Counting 2
A. 9, B. 7, C. 12, D. 11
Cauldron C has the most creatures.

**Page 92 – Spot
the Difference**

**Page 94 – Spooky
Picture Crossword**

Page 98 – Barmy Broomsticks
C

Page 100 – Find the Witch's Shadows
1. E, 2. C, 3. D, 4. B, 5. A

Page 102 – Odd One Out 2
1c, 2b, 3b, 4c

Page 104 – Cosmo Wordsnake

Start

Page 107 – Counting Kittens
11 kittens

Page 108 – Where Are the Witches?
7 with cats, 9 without cats

Page 118 – What Do They Need?
A. 1, B. 3, C. 2, D. 3

Page 120 – Odd One Out 3
Picture 2

Page 122 – Cats, bats and rats!
5 cats, 10 bats, 8 rats

Page 124 – Are You Crazy About Cosmo?
1. India, 2. Green, 3. She'd go up in a puff of smoke
4. 100, 5. Sneeze, 6. Paws, 7. A short nose, 8. Spike

A selected list of titles available from Macmillan Children's Books

The prices shown below are correct at the time of going to press. However, Macmillan Publishers reserves the right to show new retail prices on covers, which may differ from those previously advertised.

All Pan Macmillan titles can be ordered from our website, www.panmacmillan.com, or from your local bookshop and are also available by post from:

Bookpost, PO Box 29, Douglas, Isle of Man IM99 1BQ
Credit cards accepted. For details:
Telephone: 01624 677237
Fax: 01624 670923
Email: bookshop@enterprise.net
www.bookpost.co.uk